FUBAR

by Karl Gajdusek

A SAMUEL FRENCH ACTING EDITION

SAMUEL FRENCH

FOUNDED 1830

NEW YORK HOLLYWOOD LONDON TORONTO

SAMUELFRENCH.COM

ISBN 978-0-573-69792-0   Printed in U.S.A.   #29210

MUSIC USE NOTE

IMPORTANT BILLING AND CREDIT
REQUIREMENTS

FUBAR received its world premiere at Theater of Note in Los Angles, California on April 24, 2009. The play was directed by Larissa Kokernot, with sets by Gary Smoot; costumes by Joel Scher; lighting by Michael Mahlum; original music and sound by Tim Labor; projections by Darrett Sanders; and fight direction by Shawn J. Stallworth. The Production Stage Managers were Stacy Benjamin and Kelly Egan. Produced for Theatre of Note by Mark McClain Wilson. The cast was as follows:

MARY. . . . . Alice Dodd
DAVID . . . . .Ron Morehouse
RICHARD . . . . David Wilcox
SYLVIA. . . . . .Amanda Street
D.C. . . . . .Richard Werner

FUBAR was produced as a Project Y Theater Company presentation in New York City at 59E59 on June 17, 2009. The play was directed by Larissa Kokernot, with sets by Kevin Judge; costumes by Emily Pepper; lighting by Ben Hagen; original music and sound by Amit Prakash; projections by Shawn E. Boyle; and fight direction by Adam Alexander. The Production Stage Manager was John Nehlich. The cast was as follows:

MARY. . . . . Lisa Velten Smith
DAVID . . . . .Jerry Richardson
RICHARD . . . . Ryan McCarthy
SYLVIA. . . . . Stephanie Szostak
D.C. . . . . .Dan Patrick Brady

CHARACTERS

MARY – Mid-thirties. Doctor. Carries the silence of someone who grew up in another's shadow. Her mother recently took her own life, so the shadow's gone. But Mary is still quiet.

DAVID – Early thirties. Mary's husband. Exec at a nameless internet firm. Had a big exciting kick-ass plan about how this was all supposed to work. This plan should be starting any day now.

RICHARD – Mid-thirties. Charismatic, intelligent, drug-dealer. David's old friend.

SYLVIA – Late twenties. Beautiful San Francisco denizen. Outgoing and adventurous. Trying to have the biggest life possible.

D.C. – Late thirties. Boxer, retired. Old school. Lives in a different San Francisco from the others.

NOTE: Although race is not specified here, a production should take into consideration the diversity of San Francisco and the opportunities of a diverse cast.

SETTING

The living room of a San Francisco Victorian house. The room is filled with cardboard boxes, labeled somewhat cryptically by hand: "Virginity", "Bad Celebrations", "People I want to forget." Set on top of a pile, two boxes: "For Mary." "For David." Mary and David have been here for two months, camped out, living out of suitcases. A small camp stove makes the kitchen. A doorway leads outside. Across the room, an open doorway leads further into the house, but no one goes there. There is an antique make-up vanity downstage, a chair in front of it, the only sacred space here. The feeling of trespass that accompanies coming into the home of the recently departed pervades

At least two screens make up the walls of the house and on these are projected the photographic elements of the play.

Downstage, D.C.'s Boxing Gym needs only space to move in, and a worn heavy-bag, hanging. Richard and Sylvia's spaces are signified by their two personal computers.

ON DRUGS

Some of the characters in the play partake of intricate mixes of recreational drugs. The effect is in some ways the polar opposite of the slurred or spaced-out mannerism associated with being drunk or stoned. Best played very unaffected, or in careful, educated changes of manner.

1. Home

(**MARY**, *standing in front of her mother's vanity, wearing a doctor's coat.*)

(The sounds of the street.)

(She reaches forward and picks up a tin of make-up and we are...)

2. Chill Space

(Downstage, surrounded by dark, **DAVID** *and* **RICHARD**. **DAVID** *is still wearing his tie, although loosened.)*

(Near-by, **SYLVIA***, bobbing her head to electronic trance music.* **DAVID** *stares at* **SYLVIA***.)*

*(***RICHARD*** gives* **DAVID** *a series of pills which he takes or puts away as directed.)*

RICHARD. This is 5-HTP. Drop this with the C and together they'll protect the serotonin receptors from burn-out. This is milkthistle extract and B-12, which you want to put away and drop tomorrow morning. In general, if you're going to be using E, you're going to want to start taking Glutamine which provides the aminos to rebuild your brain chemistry.

DAVID. Yeah I have no idea what you're talking about. You lost me at dropping Vitamin C –

RICHARD. Drop. Take. Incorporate. With these drugs, it's not like you can self-regulate. One beer, two beers, three beers. This is different, which is where the fear comes from. Dropping is the only decision you get to make, the rest is just consequences. This is Prozac.

DAVID. It's okay. I'm not depressed.

RICHARD. It's an SSRI. Selective Serotonin Re-uptake Inhibitor. It closes down the parts of your brain that re-absorb the chemical. It's a smoother ride and the people at Stanford believe it also protects from brain damage.

*(***DAVID*** swallows the pill.)*

DAVID. God, whatever happened to just getting high? Sorry. I don't mean to be un-cool.

RICHARD. Don't worry about it. "Cool" is for alcohol or THC. This is a different process. "Cool" really has no meaning here. It's just a word, like "Democracy" or "History."

DAVID. What's on your tax return, Richard?

RICHARD. Sorry?

DAVID. Don't get me wrong. All of this is just amazing. But, you know. What do you do?

RICHARD. What do I do? What *am* I?

DAVID. Yes, what do you do?

RICHARD. I'm writing a book, about the problem of self recognition. We have this idea that we know who we are: "I am a good person." "I like internet pornography." But it's only an illusion. You wake up, you think "I am beautiful." Then you go for a piss and the mirror shows you what you really look like. Where is the mirror that shows you who you really are?

DAVID. Wow.

RICHARD. You're the perfect example. If you could be anyone in the world, be anywhere in the world, what would that be?

DAVID. I'd be...right here. I'd be...you.

RICHARD. Be serious.

DAVID. I am serious. I'd be you.

RICHARD. Alright, why aren't you me?

DAVID. I don't know.

RICHARD. Because perhaps, in your head, you're a man standing in a suburban living room, pouring coffee onto the floor.

DAVID. Okay. Wait, why am I –

RICHARD. No. Imagine it. You're an innocent, staring across the void, for the first time catching a glimpse, that there's something else out there. Something better –

DAVID. I watch my life happen.

RICHARD. – And then this one day you just know. You stop pouring the coffee onto the floor. You get a dish towel. You clean up. You take off your clothes. You walk out of the house naked and never look back. You've become a man.

(pause)

DAVID. Do you think I could slap my wife and not be…I don't know, destroyed?

RICHARD. Do you want to slap your wife?

DAVID. I really love this woman. And yet, every once in a while when she says something really degrading to me, up comes this rush of endorphins. Endorphins, right? And I just want to slap the living shit out of her. Now I will NEVER do this. I mean, there's a history with that in her family. So I don't even flinch, I don't even blink.

RICHARD. But you'll tell me about it.

DAVID. You're a drug dealer.

RICHARD. I'm –

DAVID. You're like a bartender but with a darker understanding.

RICHARD. I'm not really –

DAVID. I know. I know. It's not exactly Scarface with you.

RICHARD. No.

DAVID. *(off* **SYLVIA***)* God, that woman is just… She just exudes sexuality, don't you think? Maybe I'm…

RICHARD. Coming on?

(He checks his watch.)

No, not yet.

DAVID. "Coming on?" It's a whole new language, isn't it? And that woman, she just…glows.

(beat)

Tell me what's going to happen to me.

RICHARD. When you're in love, or when you feel pleasure, your brain produces Serotonin.

DAVID. Serotonin is happiness.

RICHARD. Serotonin is happiness. E produces Serotonin.

DAVID. And brain damage.

RICHARD. Yes, and brain damage.

DAVID. Am I going to fall in love?

RICHARD. No. But you'll be reminded of what that feels like.

(pause)

DAVID. Mary's mom killed herself. That's why we came here. We're, you know, packing up the house.

*(Beat. **RICHARD** hugs **DAVID**.)*

RICHARD. Listen to me, David. Sometimes grief can be an opportunity. They've shown that Dopamine levels significantly –

*(**DAVID** breaks away.)*

DAVID. God, listen to you. Look at you, Richard. You used to be…I mean fuck we were both just these little squirming pods hoping that something would happen to us. And to be honest, I thought it would happen to me. But it happened to you, didn't it? Something happened to you. Look at you. You have…gravitas.

RICHARD. Actually, I'm on 2CB, which is a very clear experience. And I use Ketamine, which is a dissociative, to get perspective, and a small amount of Opium to stay in touch with what's important and not over-analyze things. I'm…tuned. Like a guitar. Perfectly, in tune.

(pause)

DAVID. Fuck.

RICHARD. Don't let it freak you out. Whatever happened to just getting high, right?

DAVID. Alright, that woman is like…gravity. She's like a law of nature.

RICHARD. What about your wife?

DAVID. Mary is like…centrifugal force.

*(**DAVID** is staring at **SYLVIA**.)*

RICHARD. You think you can get lucky?

DAVID. I don't know, couldn't I always? I mean…

RICHARD. I remember.

(pause)

DAVID. No. I just want to talk to her, watch her mouth move, have a fantasy of an impossibly excellent blow-job, say nice meeting you, call it a conversation.

RICHARD. What's on your tax return, David?

> *(beat)*

DAVID. I'm a photographer.

RICHARD. Really?

DAVID. …Why not? I'm a moderately famous photographer.

RICHARD. That's amazing, David.

> *(beat)*
>
> Sylvia!
>
> *(**SYLVIA** hears, comes over.)*
>
> This is David, from high school. David, this is Sylvia, my wife. David's a photographer.

SYLVIA. That's incredible. Did Richard tell you? We've been looking for someone to do me. Actually, to do us both.

> *(beat)*

DAVID. Please don't talk right now. At. Me.

SYLVIA. I don't understand.

> *(**DAVID** closes his eyes. **RICHARD** motions her over and whispers in her ear. **SYLVIA** laughs.)*
>
> David? Open your eyes, David. Watch me.
>
> *(reciting, slowly)*
>
> *"La sottise, l'erreur, le péché, la lésine,*
> *Occupent nos esprits et travaillent nos corps."*

DAVID. Jesus…

SYLVIA. It's okay. It's Baudelaire.

> *(**SYLVIA** leans forward, and kisses **DAVID**'s forehead.)*
>
> Here, you're allowed all your imagination.
>
> *(**DAVID** glances to **RICHARD**. Brief tableau, then…)*

3. Home

(MARY, standing in front of her mother's vanity, wearing a doctor's coat.)

(She takes off the coat, drops it on the floor.)

(The sound of the street.)

(She picks up the tin of make-up from the vanity.)

(Lights shift.)

DAVID. *(hidden behind boxes)* Hey, Mary! If we see Richard at the party tonight, I'm going to try to buy some drugs of our own. I think we don't have enough drugs and we have way too much wine.

MARY. Okay.

(DAVID comes out wearing cargo pants and a T-shirt that reads "I'm not gay but my boyfriend is." He has a box with brand new $300 sneakers which he puts on.)

DAVID. Where were you last night? When I got home you weren't here. I fell asleep.

MARY. I went for a walk.

DAVID. It was really late.

MARY. There's a house that burned down. Maybe we should have a child.

DAVID. We don't want a child.

MARY. Really? Why not?

DAVID. Because we're still working on us.

MARY. Oh.

DAVID. Look, the thirties seem like a good time to become drug addicts. And Richard is really nice about it. You'll see. I mean he's always been like the nicest guy and now he's the drug-dealer but he's still like the nicest guy. And he's always talking about drugs, just like they were anything. It's like I'll say I don't like Pinot because it's for snobs and he'll say he's always felt that way about cocaine.

MARY. Look at you, you're so good at this.

DAVID. I just think we need to get under the skin. Techno music, bacchanalia, there's this society called the cacophony society. For Christmas, there's Santacide. It's a thousand Santas on Acid assaulting Macy's.

MARY. San Francisco.

DAVID. San Francisco. So if we see Richard tonight I'm going to fucking score.

MARY. If the two of you are reconnecting, maybe you shouldn't ask him for drugs.

DAVID. No, see that's the point about being a drug dealer and Richard. He's not ashamed. We're ashamed. And we're not even ashamed. But if we were, it would be our problem. You know he's married now and he's writing a book and Sylvia knows this Baudelaire poem she's – I want to say she's free or ethereal or something, but it makes her sound like a hippie.

MARY. Yes.

DAVID. I mean the rest of the world is just…off limits. And I don't want to be beheaded and I don't want you to be beheaded. Which can happen now even in France and so this…this city.

MARY. How was work?

DAVID. It's like there's a mirror. And it can show you what's inside. This city is like a mirror.

MARY. You sound like you already belong here.

DAVID. I do. I belong here.

(He moves to her and kisses her, for real. She kisses him back.)

*(**MARY** breaks the kiss. He stares at her.)*

Work was like having a screw slowly twisted into my brain until each of my limbs became weak and paralyzed and then I died.

MARY. They gave me a shift, at the hospital.

DAVID. *(beat)* Then that's it. We're here. We're really living here. We should open a box. If you're ready, we should open one of these fucking boxes. I mean it's what she must have wanted. She put these here, like this, for us. Or for you.

MARY. David –

DAVID. Sooner or later, we're going to have to…unpack.

MARY. Maybe tomorrow. Tomorrow we can –

DAVID. You took a job. I have a job. We live here. We live *here, now.* Right now.

(Beat. **MARY** *picks up a box, hands it to* **DAVID,** *moves across the room.)*

(He opens it, brings out photographs.)

(PROJECTION: "One thousand versions of me.")

MARY. What is it?

DAVID. It's just…pictures. They're all of Judith, I mean your mom. This looks like Woodstock, or I don't know, something in the park. Here, she's on the bridge. Here's both of them – do you want to see?

MARY. I don't think I'm going to go tonight.

DAVID. All right. Whatever you want.

*(***DAVID*** *starts to spread out the photographs of Mary's mother on the floor.)*

MARY. Are you going to go?

DAVID. I think it will be interesting.

MARY. Interesting. Incredible. Amazing. Fantastic. That's how she talked, do you remember? Everyone was incredible, amazing, the absolute best. We were surrounded by incredible people. And we were the luckiest people on earth to be in this amazing city and with all these amazing incredible interesting people.

*(***DAVID*** *has found a new group of photographs.)*

What?

DAVID. She's naked – nude. I mean, they're nudes of her. If you don't want me to see –

MARY. No, it's okay.

*(***DAVID*** *sets a small photo of Mary's mother up on a chair, near the opening which leads further into the house.)*

DAVID. There she is, standing right there, naked. And she doesn't even care. She's…unashamed.

(**MARY** *pulls another box out, opens it.*)

(*PROJECTION: "Something I did for another person."*)

MARY. Oh…

(**MARY** *pulls out a wedding dress. Holds it against her body in front of the vanity mirror.*)

DAVID. I think about it, how she stayed with him, all those years, and what you say she went through. You know when they say "domestic violence?" As if it was… domesticated. Like a pet.

(*beat*)

I'm just saying that for me your mom was really alive. I liked her. She was really… I'm just saying that my memories of this house are probably really different from your memories of this house.

MARY. Probably.

(*He lifts an old camera out of the box, looks at* **MARY** *through the viewfinder, clicks the shutter.*)

(*PROJECTION: The picture of* **MARY**. *It's her, although there's no way to be sure because she's in silhouette.*)

(*Beat.* **DAVID** *looks at the pictures he has laid out on the floor.*)

DAVID. Look, I won't go out, either. We can watch a DVD together –

MARY. Maybe we have to break up. Maybe we should get a divorce. If it keeps going on like this.

DAVID. I'm saying all the right things. I am. I'm saying all the right things.

MARY. I think that when someone – when you meet someone or someone you love says something to you. I think you know immediately everything. You know everything about what they really are, what they really think of you. But only for a split second. Like a flash that lingers on the back of your eye.

MARY. *(cont.)* And then all this other information comes flooding in, which is ninety percent bullshit, but it's designed to keep you from acting on what you've learned. And so, you forget.

(beat)

So when you talk to me. All I hear at first is "I hate you. You're ruining my life you worthless weight. You horrible weight."

(beat)

And then, a split second later, that fades. And there you are, saying all the right things.

DAVID. That's insane.

MARY. Don't call me insane. It's dismissive.

DAVID. That's horrible.

MARY. I know. I don't want to be horrible. I love you.

DAVID. I don't know what to say to any of that. We should have been doing what normal people do. We go through the boxes, or we don't, we throw them away, we clean up, we sell the house or move into the house or any of that. But you said no and I...respected – I have been *waiting*, for you...

(beat)

I don't know what to say to any of that.

MARY. I know. Go to the party. Do drugs.

DAVID. What have we been waiting for?

*(**MARY** turns away.)*

Mary! I'm talking to you.

(Music starts playing from somewhere. Late 60s rock ballad like Janis's "Summertime."*)

...that fucking song.

*(**DAVID** starts tearing around looking for the source of the music, listening to boxes. He's almost got it pinpointed when...it stops.)*

Fuck fuck fuck.

*See Music Use Note on page 3.

(A box falls from its perch.)

*(PROJECTION: "For **DAVID**.")*

*(Pause. They stare at it. **DAVID** opens it, reaches in. Pulls out a gun.)*

DAVID. *(cont.)* Okay, what is this? Is this some kind of supernatural threat? I mean what the fuck, Mary? That box has my name on it. What is this supposed to mean?

*(**MARY** is a million miles away. **DAVID** puts the gun back in the box.)*

Mary...You know it's not the same gun. They would have taken that one away.

MARY. I know.

(silence)

DAVID. I'm going to go to the party. Watch a DVD.

MARY. Or I might take a walk.

DAVID. It's late.

(beat)

Or take a walk. Good night.

MARY. Good night.

(He almost leaves, then.)

DAVID. Just then. When I held the camera up, and saw you through it. You looked so beautiful. And I thought to myself "Look at that. Look at the incredible woman who married me. Everything is right. Everything makes sense."

MARY. When you're threatened, you become so nice. Why do you do that?

(beat)

DAVID. Good night, Mary.

(He leaves. She stares after him. Then she stares at her mother's vanity.)

(Carefully, she sits at the vanity. She picks up the same tin of make-up.)

(The sound of the street.)

MARY. I walked up through the panhandle and I turned up Cole. I was thinking I might get one of those delicious wraps. I took a small detour to see this house which had been gutted by fire the week before.

(She opens the tin. It's dark make-up.)

I was standing across the street, looking up at the house. Plywood was nailed across the windows. It looked wounded and sad and empty.

(She laughs to herself, small and private.)

He hit me from behind and since I was standing in front of a car, I fell into it and I caught the rim of the roof in my teeth before I went down.

Thinking…God, what was I thinking? Thinking "nothing caused this. This is just happening."

(She begins to make herself up.)

He was screaming at me. I got up, because it seemed hard to communicate from the ground. And I wanted to give him my wallet so he would stop, and I had to make this point.

As soon as I stood up, he threw a high left hook and I caught it with my shoulder and I almost fell again, but I didn't. I tried to hit him back. I didn't know how to hit so I wound up pushing at him, breaking one of my fingers. He pushed me back away from him against the car, and I thought well now that's over. But then he came back.

He came back like the weather.

Right uppercut, into my rib cage and he cracked two of my ribs and took my air. Tight left hook, he hit me in the face and dislocated my jaw and I fell back and his right followed and broke my nose and split my cheek. Three of my teeth shattered.

Later, much later, I would figure out all of these details. I would learn the words for my own destruction, and rebuilding. But at the time, there was only relief. I

lay there, my face in the gutter, the cool water running over my ruined cheek. And there was only relief.
Thinking, "Is that it?" "Is that it?"

(**MARY** *has finished making herself up. Her face is a
calm disaster. All the damage she just described.*)

4. Hospital

(**MARY** *is in the hospital bed.*)

(**DAVID** *can't sit still, he's like a child's fist.*)

(**MARY***'s jaw is swollen, painful to talk, but not too hard.*)

DAVID. You're going to be fine. They've told you that, right? Everything's fine and actually, there's kind of a list I was thinking about.

(**DAVID** *takes out a piece of paper, reads.*)

First of all, you're going to be fine.

Secondly, I love you.

Thirdly, it could have been worse.

Fourthly, or fourth. I'm here. There's me.

That's it. That's the list. It seemed better when I thought of it that way.

How do you feel?

MARY. …Good.

DAVID. Good?

MARY. When I was actually getting hit –

DAVID. That fucking asshole. Fuck!

MARY. I was thinking: "This is a guy, punching me. David can hurt me worse than this. David has hurt me worse than this."

(*pause*)

DAVID. I don't know what to say to that.

MARY. You, can hurt me, because I love you. All he could do, was…injure me. That's…Good. It's good.

DAVID. Fuck. I can't believe this. Fuck.

(*pause*)

MARY. This is hard for you.

DAVID. I'm sorry.

MARY. The police think he broke his hand. Because that's what happens. The small bones in the hand, when they hit the bones in my face. I mean, if they hit –

DAVID. Okay. Okay.

(silence)

I told Richard, and Sylvia. They're…horrified. And they want to help, if they can.

(She looks at him. Nods.)

I told them about how you looked through the camera. You know ever since finding that camera I've been thinking a lot about taking pictures.

(pause)

MARY. I bet she would pose nude for you.

DAVID. Who? What? Fuck. Why?

MARY. It's San Francisco.

(pause)

DAVID. Well, it's not that interesting to me…I mean I'm not a prude. It's not like I don't think it would be interesting…I guess it would be fun. But I was thinking, I want to take your picture. Like this.

MARY. I don't know if I want that.

DAVID. I know.

(MARY has a small mirror tucked in the blankets. She takes it out, looks at herself.)

MARY. I don't want to be "mauled woman." I don't want to be that.

DAVID. Of course.

MARY. There was already a detective, taking pictures. And then the doctor's…

DAVID. *(gently)* So there is something bad about this.

(pause)

Did you see him?

MARY. Yes, a little. His face. I'd know if I saw it again.

DAVID. I'd kill him. If I knew who he was, I'd kill him.

MARY. No. He's not yours. He's mine.

(pause)

DAVID. I do love you.

MARY. So why do you want a picture of this?

(beat)

David?

DAVID. I don't know. Please.

*(**DAVID** opens his bag, pulls out the camera. He waits.)*

MARY. Okay.

(She turns her face up to him. He starts taking pictures.)

*(On the screens, portraits of **MARY**, her face bruised and broken.)*

(Then they fade, one by one, replaced by…)

5. Home

(DAVID is taking pictures of SYLVIA.)

SYLVIA. The whole thing started out in the 80's with Sim-City, just grew from there. Sim-Railroad, Sim-World, all these non-violent simulation games and then the internet and that was it, Sim Life and now we were really dealing with real people in this unreal world and so who was to say what the borders of reality were then?

(DAVID takes a picture.)

DAVID. Why don't you take your hair down?

SYLVIA. But I was telling *no one* I was into it, because man you think there's a stigma around those things for men. We're not supposed to be virtual, just…"real," which is another word for vagina. But even when I was little I was like "fuck reality."

DAVID. Maybe we should –

SYLVIA. And Richard did Ashtanga and I had been thinking about Bikhram and he pointed out the fascism there – he has this information like that, he's this great boy-friend or "husband." But there was this void between us which we could both sense. Like we were living in a silent movie. I mean, we were talking, but we weren't actually *speaking*. To each other. You can ask me to do something.

DAVID. Can you look down, and then, when I say, look up at me.

(SYLVIA looks down.)

SYLVIA. And we would go home and do all that sex and fine but there was this other level, just beneath the skin, or the moment we were sharing. Because we both–

DAVID. Look up.

(She doesn't.)

SYLVIA. We both were dreaming about that unreal person waiting for us online. I mean there we are in bed, fuck-ing each other's brains out, I mean "ah ah ah!"…

(He takes a picture.)

SYLVIA. *(cont.)* …and it's skin and saliva and you know, your muscles. And we're both secretly waiting to get back, to this –

DAVID. Let's try that again.

SYLVIA. This other, anonymous, virtual person that, at least sexually…

DAVID. Look up. Please.

(She doesn't.)

SYLVIA. And so one night, he was lying on me, inside of me, and I just said, "Have you ever done this online?" And he got really really still.

DAVID. Look up.

(She does. He takes a picture.)

SYLVIA. Do you want me to take off my shirt? I mean, I don't mind.

DAVID. That would be great.

(She does, bra underneath. He takes a picture.)

What happened then?

SYLVIA. He told me yes. One word. And he smiled. And in that instant I knew it was him. I knew that the naked man lying on top of me, and the man I had met online, were the same man. Ahmed Kahn. Kahn. Richard was AhmedKahn248.

DAVID. Look at me. Right now. Look at me.

(She does. He shoots.)

SYLVIA. And we realized that this was, you know, entirely transcendental. Both of us. Both places. Here. There. Double the life.

DAVID. Look at me again.

SYLVIA. And it's two sides. There's Richard who is smart and has all these high-grade pharmaceuticals. And then there's Ahmed Kahn, who only lives in the glow of the computer screen and can give me an orgasm

SYLVIA. *(cont.)* just by you know: ampersand, ampersand, ampersand over and over. And they are the same man. Different, but the same man. Do you see? The Tibetans and the Kabbalah all have this variation on reincarnation where souls come back and you don't have to really even believe just accept the possibility that through this system, through this consensual internet hallucination we're finally getting more life and I don't mean a longer life I mean more, more life.

(beat)

DAVID. What's your online name?

SYLVIA. Rocket Twat. Ahmed Kahn, and Rocket Twat. I know.

DAVID. San Francisco.

SYLVIA. It's amazing, don't you think?

DAVID. Amazing.

(beat)

What happened, once you both knew?

*(**SYLVIA** takes off her pants.)*

SYLVIA. Sometimes, I see it in his eyes. If things have gotten really intense or hardcore online, he'll come into the room, he'll wink, or laugh…

DAVID. He may not know.

SYLVIA. No. He's letting me know he knows.

DAVID. I don't mean to…you know. But what if he doesn't? What if he just thinks that you…that Rocket Twat is just…someone he met online.

SYLVIA. *(beat)* Then I guess he's just cheating on me.

DAVID. On you…with you.

SYLVIA. You see! Isn't it amazing?

DAVID. Look at me.

(She does. He takes a picture.)

Fuck!

(beat)

DAVID. *(cont.)* I don't actually know people like you. I know that's stupid to say…

(beat)

The other night with Richard. When you came over, and you were just stunning. And now you're here you're right here. And if I could just…capture any of that…

SYLVIA. How long have you been here?

DAVID. We've been here two months.

SYLVIA. Two months, you're taking pictures of a woman in her underwear. You're totally on track. You're going to do well here.

(her bra)

Do you want me to take this off?

DAVID. No.

SYLVIA. Okay.

(brief pause)

God, I feel like I just got turned down at the prom.

DAVID. I'm sorry. Me, too.

*(**DAVID** changes film. **SYLVIA** moves to the vanity and chair.)*

SYLVIA. This is where she killed herself, isn't it?

DAVID. Yes.

*(**SYLVIA** starts to slide the chair out to sit.)*

Actually, don't do that.

(She stops. Instead she puts her hands on the back of the chair and closes her eyes.)

Mary's mother was…She was really something. We used to visit and she would tell us these stories about San Francisco. She was…I guess she was a hippie. She was always talking like "Hey, man. Isn't this food wonderful? Isn't this view amazing? Isn't it all incredible, man?"

DAVID. *(cont.)* Her, um, her husband was really different, really not part of that. I never met him but I think she, she was love and he was…he wasn't.

> *(beat)*

> Look, if you're channeling or something then I wish you wouldn't do that.

> *(SYLVIA opens her eyes.)*

SYLVIA. Okay.

> *(DAVID takes a picture.)*

> How is your wife?

DAVID. She's going to be alright. She comes home tomorrow.

SYLVIA. I think about it all the time now. I mean, I'm so stupid, because I thought that women got, you know, raped. And that men got beat up.

DAVID. Try kneeling.

SYLVIA. See, you're getting braver.

> *(She kneels. He takes a picture.)*

DAVID. Help me.

> *(silence)*

SYLVIA. I think you know what you want, you just can't say the words. Because maybe what you want, the picture you want, isn't such a nice thing to take. But that's what we like about you, David. Nice is for the rest of the world. This doesn't have to be nice.

> *(Beat. DAVID goes to the "For David" box and gives it to her. She pulls out the gun. She holds it in front of her, doesn't know what to do with it.)*

> *(DAVID picks up the camera. Click. Click. From somewhere in the boxes, the 60's song plays.)*

DAVID. That fucking song…

> *(DAVID starts looking for the source of the music. MARY comes in. She wears a long sleeve shirt. She and SYLVIA stare at each other.)*

(Just as **DAVID***'s about to pinpoint it, the music stops.* **DAVID** *sees* **MARY***.)*

DAVID. *(cont.)* You're home. That's supposed to be tomorrow.

MARY. I checked myself out early.

DAVID. There's a woman in her underwear in our home.

SYLVIA. Hi.

MARY. Yes there is. It's okay, David.

DAVID. I know it's okay. I know it's totally fine. But somehow, I don't think it's okay. This is Sylvia.

*(***SYLVIA*** puts down the gun, starts getting dressed.* **MARY** *looks at the gun, then at* **SYLVIA***.)*

MARY. David's told me so much about both of you.

SYLVIA. Yes. I'm really sorry about what happened to you.

MARY. Well...I'm home, now.

(Beat. The pictures **DAVID** *just took of* **SYLVIA** *play back on the screens in fast succession.)*

6. The Gym

(D.C. attacks the Heavy Bag.)

(MARY watches him. Long sleeve shirt.)

(Finally, he's done. He backs off, breathing hard. He turns around. They stare at each other across the gym.)

MARY. My name is Mary Conrad.

(pause)

D.C.. What do you want?

(She points at the heavy bag.)

(He starts to walk towards her. She puts up her hand, to shield her face, just a little. He stops.)

It's not for sale.

MARY. That's not what I meant.

D.C.. I know what you meant.

(beat)

No matter what you do, you will never be able to stop someone like me. You know that, right? You see that film?

MARY. No.

D.C.. You sure? It was a good movie.

MARY. No.

D.C.. So what do you want?

MARY. I want to hit someone. I want to know how to hit someone.

D.C.. You want to hit a person, or hurt a person?

MARY. Yes. Both.

D.C.. You couldn't hurt a person.

MARY. *(hard)* Look at my face.

(He does. Then he turns away.)

D.C.. That's not my problem.

MARY. I can pay you.

D.C.. You know how many women come in here just like you? It's like every week these days. They see that movie. It's like it's raining women these days.

MARY. They can't all be like me.

D.C.. No, they're good looking. You're not so good looking anymore.

MARY. A man did this to me.

D.C.. I know, I saw on the TV. Why do you think he did that to you?

MARY. I don't know. I mean, I guess he was…sad.

D.C.. Looks more like angry to me.

MARY. Of course, that. But I guess, underneath –

D.C.. No, that's bullshit. He was just pissed off. He's not thinking about you. You got any kids?

MARY. No. Do you?

D.C.. You married?

MARY. Yes.

D.C.. Your husband, he must have been pretty mad.

MARY. No…I think he was just upset.

D.C.. Oh. So that's why you think your guy was sad. Because your husband is like that.

(brief pause)

MARY. Yes. Maybe that's right. Please.

D.C.. Come here.

*(Beat. **MARY** comes close.)*

Let me see your hands.

*(**MARY** puts out her hands.)*

(He takes them in his, turns them palm upwards, then starts to build fists.)

Here, you close these first. Tight. Good. Then you take this, tuck it here.

(off her thumb)

You let this out, it'll break right off. You understand?

MARY. Yes.

(He's still holding her hands.)

D.C.. Good. Don't do this too hard, you'll hurt your wrist.

*(He lets go of her hands. Beat. **MARY** hits the heavy bag. A slight SLAP to the sound.)*

7. Home

(**SYLVIA** *lies on the bed.*)

(**RICHARD** *sits in front of* **DAVID***'s open powerbook, studying the screen.*)

(*Across the room,* **DAVID** *sits with his camera. He takes pictures of* **RICHARD***. Restless.*)

RICHARD. So that's really it then? The internet?

(**DAVID** *takes a picture.*)

DAVID. That's the raw data. I mean, a tiny piece of it. My company makes the switches, the things that tell it all where to go.

RICHARD. Wow.

DAVID. Most of it is porn. Shopping. Junk. Most of it is porn.

(**DAVID** *takes a picture.*)

RICHARD. You're not really a photographer, are you David?

(**DAVID** *takes a picture. Another. Sets the camera down.*)

Well don't worry. Maybe you're a photographer, who just hasn't realized that yet.

DAVID. You know you weren't always on drugs. I remember...

RICHARD. Serotonin, Noradrenaline, Dopamine. These are the chemicals that make up the brain, David. We can't really choose to be "on" or "off" these things. We are these things.

DAVID. What about now?

RICHARD. Three milligrams of Psilocybin for an open mind. Dissolved in an amphetamine tea which keeps it from getting sloppy and then there's a small amount of GHB to elicit mischief or humor.

DAVID. What am I on?

RICHARD. Fear.

DAVID. Excuse me?

RICHARD. Well, what I *gave you* was 5-methoxy-N N-diiso-propyltryptamine, otherwise known as Foxy. But if we take a second to look at you, David…you're not very foxy. Instead, you seem to be wrestling with what I call a kill/fuck instinct. If you can't kill it, fuck it. If you can't fuck it, kill it. Kill. Fuck. Kill. Fuck. Primal stuff, baby.

DAVID. Don't…reduce everything.

RICHARD. Basis of western civilization. Now where's the capsule I gave you?

(Beat. **DAVID** *produces the pill he palmed and sets it on the table in front of him.)*

Are you scared of brain damage?

DAVID. Yes.

RICHARD. Go to the playground and look at that one kid with no friends, or maybe one friend. He can't speak. He can't look other people in the eyes. He's lost the motor skills necessary for sincere laughter. You don't think that fear, and loneliness – that regret and self-loathing – you don't think these things do lasting damage? Brain damage is a by-product of being alive, David.

DAVID. *(beat, then off* **SYLVIA***)* What's she on?

RICHARD. Sylvia's in a K-hole. Ketamine. She's actually very much with us right now, but not there…in her body. She's…

(pointing around)

Out there, watching us, watching herself. I injected her with seventy-five milligrams of –

DAVID. You *injected* her? You see, Richard, I can't do this. Why do you do this? To be totally honest I don't know what this is.

RICHARD. Do you like Sir Francis Drake?

DAVID. I fucking *love* Sir Francis Drake.

RICHARD. Okay, you're Sir Francis Drake, exploring the new world. And well, you're done, so now you're Louis and Clark, heading into the West. And well, you get there. So now you're Neil Armstrong, stepping onto the moon and fuck shit god damn you're there. You're standing on the moon.

(pointing at his own head)

Undiscovered country. Final frontier. We've filled up and fucked up every place out there. Only one place left with unspoiled land.

DAVID. Mary's started boxing.

RICHARD. You see?! Soldiers, coming back from war with PTSD. Car backfires, recalls the traumatic event and just lays them down. Yet sure enough, they search out places with loud noises.

DAVID. No, that's not it. It's for self defense.

RICHARD. This is actually what I'm writing about. Who we are, what are the boxes that define us, or confine us. By the way have you noticed, David, that you live totally surrounded and fucking penned in by a dead woman's boxes?

DAVID. Yeah, I noticed.

RICHARD. You're living in a life-sized etymology, a sum total history and derivation, of this woman. And now your wife has a box called "Man hitting me." How do you think she's going to open that box? By going back to it. By being hit. People think drugs are addictive, try love, try violence, try living.

DAVID. That's not –

RICHARD. Try "Ooooo! I saw daddy on top of mommy!"

DAVID. How much –

RICHARD. Try "Oooo! My best friend steals my girlfriends."

DAVID. How much do they pay you?

RICHARD. There's even dealers, who we call therapists. And then there's the supply chain which we call Viacom and Clearchanel, bringing you daily re-enactments of

trauma and heartbreak all directed right at your heav-
ily addicted…heart.

(RICHARD *pokes* DAVID *in the chest.*)

DAVID. I make six figures. I make six fucking figures.

RICHARD. I'm impressed.

DAVID. No, you're not impressed. But you should be. It's hard.

RICHARD. Let me suggest something to you. You're a drug
addict, addicted to a powerful narcotic called "really
living." Which is defined, by you, as the exact opposite
of whatever your life, your normal living, is. See Sylvia
and I gave you a taste of this "really living" and now
your normal everyday life seems bland and unfulfilling
and now you'll do anything to get more of this "real
life." You don't believe me? Of course not, you're a
drug addict. Drug addicts are in denial. And the only
way to know what you really want…

(RICHARD *points at* SYLVIA.)

Is to get perspective. Is to take a scary illegal drug in
your arm and journey to an undiscovered country
called "you." And to answer your question, there is no
"they" to pay me. It's *my book.* It's *MINE.* Now let me ask
you a question: When are we going to open all of these
motherfucking boxes?

(*beat*)

It's been months now, hasn't it?

DAVID. Just…go home. What do you want from me?

RICHARD. What do you think I want? You are a bug. I want
to see the butterfly.

(*beat*)

DAVID. Open a box.

RICHARD. Only if you're okay with it, Foxy.

DAVID. Fuck you. Open a box.

(RICHARD *grabs a box and spills out an assortment of
unforgivable tschotchkes.*)

(*PROJECTION: "Unforgivable tchotchkes."*)

I didn't steal your girlfriends. Your girlfriends came to me. Because you were weak.

RICHARD. See? There you go. Kill kill kill.

(**RICHARD** *grabs another box, opens it. Lifts out paper napkins with writing scrawled on them.*)

(*PROJECTION: "Bad poems from good men."*)

DAVID. They only slept with you, to get near me. You were a freak.

RICHARD. Fuck fuck fuck. Kill kill kill. You're like a case study –

DAVID. Fuck you. Open another box.

(**RICHARD** *pulls over a box.*)

(*PROJECTION: "In case of emergency."*)

You *confused* people.

(**RICHARD** *reaches into the box, pulls out a music box.*)

RICHARD. Kill fuck kill fuck. It *is* confusing. Open a box, open yourself, open your heart, open your mind...

DAVID. Don't push me, Richard. I'll win.

(**RICHARD** *opens the lid and a little tune comes out. They stand there, staring at each other.*)

(*On the bed,* **SYLVIA** *starts to cry.*)

(**RICHARD** *goes to* **SYLVIA**, *tries to take her in his arms. She resists, cries more.*)

RICHARD. Sylvia. You're okay. You're just having unexpected emotions. Sylvia.

(**SYLVIA** *cries even more.*)

DAVID. Why's she crying? Is that normal?

RICHARD. Sylvia? Sylvia, I'm right here. Stop it.

DAVID. Stop it? What do you mean? I thought you knew –

(*WHAM!* **SYLVIA** *seems to convulse. Scary, hard.* **RICHARD** *goes to her, she lurches free.*)

RICHARD. It's not normal, okay? Ketamine is a paralytic. This dose should inhibit the major muscle groups –

(*WHAM! WHAM!* **SYLVIA**'s *body goes through shocks.*

RICHARD *gets her, holds her tight, intense. Staying in her face even though her eyes are closed.)*

RICHARD. *(cont.)* Sylvia! Sylvia! I'm here, baby. I'm right here. We're going to do this together –

DAVID. *(simultaneous)* O FUCK O FUCK O FUCK! WE HAVE TO CALL THE PARAMEDICS WE NEED TO CALL THE FUCKING PARAMEDICS OH MY GOD!! HELP! HELP! HELP!

(WHAM! Another terrible convulsion.)

RICHARD. SYLVIA!

*(**SYLVIA**'s eyes open. She pulls away from **RICHARD**, finally gets to the music box. Holds it tight.)*

DAVID. Judith, Mary's mom, her husband gave that to her. She told me the whole story. Because he wasn't the kind of man who would give you something like that. They had a fight, because she liked dancing and he thought... She had been dancing and he had gotten angry. But then he felt so wrong, that he bought that for her, and opened it...

(She opens it. Little tune.)

And this one time, he danced with her, right in the park, right in front of everyone.

*(**SYLVIA** smiles at **DAVID**. **RICHARD**, approaches scared. He puts his arms around **SYLVIA**, shuts the lid of the music box.)*

(Lights fade to...)

8. Mary's Walk

(**MARY** *wears a long sleeve sweat shirt. Sweat pants. Sneakers.*)

MARY. I walked up through the panhandle and I turned up Cole. I was thinking I might get one of those delicious wraps. I took a small detour to see this house which had been gutted by fire the week before.

(*The sounds of the street.*)

I was standing across the street, looking up at the house. Plywood was nailed across the windows. It looked dead and sad and empty. I stood there.

Waiting. Waiting. Waiting.

And then I went home. These people were in my house. They were all asleep. David was curled between them like a baby.

(**MARY** *quietly goes to a suitcase, gets some clean clothing.*)

(**DAVID** *wakes up. Looks around, confused. Sees her.*)

DAVID. Hey.

MARY. Hey.

DAVID. Where have you been?

MARY. …Movie.

DAVID. Okay.

(*beat*)

We had an interesting night. It's hard to explain.

MARY. You don't have to explain.

(*beat*)

DAVID. What do you remember?

MARY. …I didn't see him. So I don't really –

DAVID. No, I mean, about here. About your home.

(*beat*)

MARY. I remember her sitting at this table, and reaching into her mouth, and pulling out a tooth. I think he had pushed her into the door.

DAVID. I'm sorry. It's not what I remember. I remember the first night you brought me here, right after your dad's funeral. And she was drinking tequilla.

MARY. She put the tooth in a plastic bag, for the dentist.

DAVID. And she told me about the time that they went down under the Golden Gate and they all took off their clothes and swam in the Bay.

MARY. And then she…made up her face.

(beat)

DAVID. Well, I'm sure you're right. But I think they were happy. Don't you remember that?

(Pause. MARY starts to leave.)

Richard thinks you might have post traumatic stress disorder. He thinks you're obsessed with what happened to you. Where are you going?

MARY. Gym.

DAVID. No, it's too late. The gym is closed.

MARY. On the way, I stop where I was attacked. Tell Richard, he'll love it.

DAVID. You know, you're never home. Can I help you? I'll help you. Just tell me what you're doing.

MARY. Do you want to know what I hear you saying?

DAVID. I want to be there for you.

MARY. See, that's nice. But I hear: "What the fuck is your problem? You crazy bitch. Give me respect or I'll choke the life out of you."

(DAVID stares at her, horrified.)

If you want to help me, just be who you really are. Because this person…

(She points at him.)

I can't trust this person.

DAVID. It's not fair. This is me. *This* is how I am. I'm a good person. Look at me.

(**MARY** *throws clothes in a bag to go.* **DAVID** *finds the music box, opens it. Little tune.* **MARY** *stares at it.*)

(*PROJECTION: "In case of Emergency."*)

MARY. She...

(*Beat. This is hard. A first time.*)

He was angry and she laughed at him and he broke her wrist. The next day, he brought her that box. And she said why? Which was hopeful. And he said "The next time you want to open your mouth, you open that instead. Then we'll be okay."

(*beat*)

She threw it back at him, caught him in the cheek, drew some blood.

DAVID. That's not what she told me.

MARY. I know. I know what she told you.

(**DAVID** *stands there with the music box.* **MARY** *leaves to...*)

9. The Gym

(**MARY** *and* **D.C.**, *sparring. It's been a while. She's good. They bob, duck, block.*)

D.C.. Hit.

Hit.

Now defend.

(**MARY** *blocks blocks ducks blocks.*)

Good!

MARY. How you like me now, mutherfucker?

D.C.. Now you're all ghetto?

(**D.C.** *hits,* **MARY** *leans out, comes back in. Hits hits hits.*)

MARY. Float like a butterfly, sting like a bee.

D.C.. Watch. No, you gotta see all of me. Soft eyes. Soft eyes.

(**MARY** *hits, hits.* **D.C.** *comes around with a sneaky hook, catches her in the ribs. She stumbles back, winded.*)

(*smiling*) How you like me now?

MARY. I didn't...I didn't see that coming.

D.C.. You're looking in the wrong place. You're looking in my eyes.

(*pointing to his eyes*)

These, they'll tell you all kinds of information you don't need. Am I a good person? Maybe I'm sexy, maybe I'm lying to you. For all that, you gotta look a man in the eyes. None of that matters here.

(*tapping his sternum*)

You look here. You let your eyes stay soft, you see the whole body. You gotta see the feet, the arms. You gotta see the body, not the man. Doesn't matter who the man is.

MARY. Trust me, it matters.

D.C.. No, it doesn't. It doesn't matter.

*(Beat. **MARY** raises her gloves to begin again. They begin. **MARY** stays out of his eyes.)*

Hit. Hit!

HIT! Yes. HIT HIT BLOCK DUCK DUCK CROSS CROSS. DEFEND! DEFEND.

(He comes at her, she wraps up tight, takes the hits.)

NOW BACK IN JAB JAB JAB JAB CROSS UPPERCUT CROSS CROSS! DEFEND! DEFEND! DEFEND!

*(But **MARY** is just on a punching spree. **D.C.** clinches her, wraps her up in his arms.)*

Stop! STOP! STOP!

*(**MARY** backs off, frustrated.)*

Now you're hitting angry.

MARY. I am angry.

D.C.. You hit like you're angry with yourself.

MARY. Well, that's good, right?

D.C.. No. It's not good.

MARY. You said, use emotion, use your heart. That's it. That's heart.

D.C.. Everything wants to move, all at once. Your head, your arms, your legs, your body. They're all gonna jump forward.

MARY. Yes.

D.C.. That's not it. You make a decision. You will hit this man. So you use your toes. You use your legs, then your body, in this order, then your arms, then your fist. In that order. One after the other. Building. Because you want this man to understand. Because you want him to know, that you are here.

*(**MARY** laughs.)*

Did I say something funny?

MARY. No, not at all. Whatever you say, Confuscious.

D.C.. You're making fun?

MARY. I want him to "know that I am here?" What is that? The man who attacked me, I don't think he wanted me to "know he was there." He wanted to end my life.

D.C.. That didn't happen.

MARY. No.

D.C.. So now you know he's there.

MARY. Fuck you.

*(Beat. **D.C.** Goes back into stance.)*

D.C.. Hit. Good! Defend. Hit. Hit. HIT!

(She hits three times, very strong. He comes back at her.)

(Without warning, she drops her guard, moving into the hit so that he catches her hard across the face. She goes down.)

Why did you do that?! You dropped your guard. WHY DID YOU DO THAT?!

*(**MARY** picks herself up, shakes it off.)*

Why did you do that?

MARY. *(mocking)* "To make you know I was here."

D.C.. You want to make me know that, you break MY nose. You bust MY rib. *You* attack *me*.

*(**MARY** goes back into a fighting stance. They start sparring again, carefully.)*

MARY. Maybe I can't do that. Maybe I could train for years, and never do that.

D.C.. You got some talent.

MARY. Some talent? Have you looked at yourself in the mirror. I got some "talent?" You're like…the definition of violence. Look at yourself. You're not even human. You're like some animal. You said it yourself. How could I protect myself from an animal like you? Look at you. Just muscles and testosterone. You got a few wise words, so you can pretend to be a person. But that's bullshit. Animal. Animal. Fucking animal.

*(**D.C.** stops moving. **MARY** stops moving, but she keeps her guard up.)*

D.C.. What are you doing here?

MARY. Fuck you. Animal. Inhuman animal. Nothing.

(**MARY** *lowers her guard, as before.*)

(*They stand there, staring at each other.*)

(**D.C.** *catches her with a left hook, sending her to the ground. She spits a little blood, stands back up, ready again.*)

D.C.. We're done. This is over.

MARY. No. Please, don't. Come on! COME ON!

(*beat*)

D.C.. This is over.

(*He walks off.*)

10. Mary's Walk

(**MARY**, *fast, impatient.*)

MARY. *(fast, rote)* I walked up through the panhandle and I turned up Cole. I was thinking I might get one of those delicious wraps. I took a small detour to see this house which had been gutted by fire the week before.
(beat)

(fast, rote) I was standing across the street, looking up at the house. Plywood was nailed across the windows. It looked dead and sad and empty.

(Beat. She slows into it.)

(The sounds of the street.)

A woman approached down the block. Small, thin, that perfect hair. I thought for a moment I recognized her. When she saw me, she started to cross the street, then stopped. She passed me, giving me a little room. She was scared.

I started to follow her. She sensed it, like any woman would. I walked in her invisible footsteps. We passed under street lights. She touched her hair, glanced back. I'm sure her gender signals were all mixed up.

I would grab her, throw her against the car. Strong, cross-body blows to the ribs. She'd be protecting her face, leaving the body open for me.

(pause)

I stood there, under the lights. The woman kept moving, turned up a street, and was gone.

At home, David was fixed to his computer, blue light on his face.

(**MARY** *walks up to the vanity, looks down at the empty chair in front of it.*)

She smiles back up at me from my memory. That smile...

Hey, mom.

MARY. *(cont.)* What are you smiling about? Because I didn't make your mistakes, and I'm not smiling. And all this not smiling I'm doing, it's not an attractive quality.

Stop smiling. Stop smiling because I'll slap that smile right off your face.

Why were you happy?

I'm really trying to understand. I really want to know how you did it.

How were you so happy?

(Lights fade…)

Intermission

11. Internet

(**SYLVIA** and **RICHARD**, both on their computers. They face each other so their monitors face away. **SYLVIA** glances over at him sometimes.)

(Tap tap tap tap tap go the keys. **RICHARD** is writing his book. **SYLVIA** is sending out electronic feelers for Ahmed Kahn. Except where noted, the conversation is silent, projected.)

SYLVIA. ROCKET_TWAT: Kahn? I'm waiting for you, Kahn. <enter>

(**SYLVIA** looks over. **RICHARD** types. **SYLVIA** waits.)

ROCKET_TWAT: Kahn? Kahn? This is your Rocket Twat. Waiting. <enter>

(**SYLVIA** waits. **RICHARD** types again.)

(Lights rise on **DAVID**. He holds a vial of powder to his nose and sniffs.)

(She coughs. **RICHARD** glances over. **SYLVIA** gives him a look. He types.)

(**DAVID** types.)

DAVID. AHMED_KAHN248: Rocket? <enter>

(**SYLVIA** looks over at **RICHARD**. He doesn't look up.)

SYLVIA. ROCKET_TWAT: Kahn!!!!!!!!!!!!!! <enter>

(beat)

ROCKET_TWAT: Where have you been?????? <enter>

DAVID. AHMED_KAHN248: I know. I'm sorry. I was… marauding, in Europe. <enter>

SYLVIA. ROCKET_TWAT: Funny. Touch me. <enter>

DAVID. AHMED_KAHN248: Yes. <enter>

SYLVIA. ROCKET_TWAT: Touch me touch me touch me! <enter>

(**RICHARD** types a flurry of words.)

DAVID. AHMED_KAHN248: Yes! <enter>

(**SYLVIA** *looks at* **RICHARD***, confused by the disparity.*)

SYLVIA. ROCKET_TWAT: Are you doing two things at once? <enter>

(beat)

DAVID. AHMED_KAHN248: Does it matter? <enter>

SYLVIA. ROCKET_TWAT: No, you're right. (sorry) Start over. I've been dying for you. I'm all alone, out here, in space. I want you to have me. Take me. <enter>

(**RICHARD** *leans back from his computer.*)

ROCKET_TWAT: Take me now. <enter>

(**RICHARD** *gets up from his computer, exits.* **SYLVIA** *watches him go, confused.*)

(**DAVID** *stares at his computer, unsure.*)

(**SYLVIA** *waits.* **DAVID** *types.*)

DAVID. AHMED_KAHN248: I fuck you, I throw you down on the hood of your space ship and rip off your circuit boards and your tits and your face are exposed below me. My hands are on your cunt and in your ass and I'm looking down at you and fucking you and god I haven't been this hard in so long.

(**DAVID***'s hand hovers over the "enter" key. Then he starts deleting what he wrote.*)

(**RICHARD** *comes back into the room with a RedBull. He puts it by the computer, types.*)

AHMED_KAHN248: Yes, I'm ready. <enter>

SYLVIA. ROCKET_TWAT: Take off my clothes. <enter>

DAVID. AHMED_KAHN248: I rip them off, with my scimitar, I'm unstoppable. <enter>

SYLVIA. ROCKET_TWAT: Yes. What do you see? <enter>

DAVID. AHMED_KAHN248: You. Your beautiful fucking body. <enter>

SYLVIA. ROCKET_TWAT: I pull away your furs. I see you, too. Your cock. <enter>

DAVID. AHMED_KAHN248: Yes. <enter>

SYLVIA. ROCKET_TWAT: YES! I need you inside me. <enter>

DAVID. AHMED_KAHN248: & & &…<enter>

SYLVIA. ROCKET_TWAT: Oh God. <enter>

DAVID. AHMED_KAHN248: & & &…<enter><enter>

SYLVIA. ROCKET_TWAT: What do you want me to do? <enter>

(**RICHARD** *lets loose a long stream of writing.*)

ROCKET_TWAT: Oh my God. <enter>

DAVID. AHMED_KAHN248: I want you to…<enter>

SYLVIA. ROCKET_TWAT: Say it. <enter>

(**RICHARD** *is still typing like mad.*)

ROCKET_TWAT: Say it. You can say it. <enter>

(**RICHARD** *stops.*)

DAVID. AHMED_KAHN248: I want you…to be with him. <enter>

SYLVIA. ROCKET_TWAT: Him? <enter>

DAVID. AHMED_KAHN248: David. <enter>

(*Pause. They all stare at their screens.*)

SYLVIA. ROCKET_TWAT: What about this? <enter>

(*pause*)

DAVID. AHMED_KAHN248: This…is just the fucking internet. <enter>

(**SYLVIA** *stares at* **RICHARD**. *He types.*)

SYLVIA. (*spoken*) Richard…

(**RICHARD** *glances up. He rises, crosses to her, his attention on his work. He gives her a kiss. Goes back to his computer.*)

ROCKET_TWAT: I would do anything for you. <enter>

DAVID. AHMED_KAHN248: Then be with him. <enter>

(**DAVID** *pushes back from the computer, spooked.*)

SYLVIA. ROCKET_TWAT: ….Richard. <enter>

(Just as **SYLVIA** *hits 'enter',* **RICHARD** *closes his computer.)*

(He laughs slightly to himself, a little personal joke.)

RICHARD. Sushi?

SYLVIA. ...I'm supposed to do more pictures with David, tomorrow night.

RICHARD. Good.

SYLVIA. You could come over, near the end.

RICHARD. Good. Sushi?

SYLVIA. Okay. If that's what you want.

(Lights shift to...)

12. Home

*(**MARY** comes in, dressed in more clothing under her doctor's coat. Sweats, a cap. **DAVID** closes his powerbook, fast.)*

*(**DAVID** watches as **MARY** hangs up her doctor's coat.)*

DAVID. She didn't know what she was going to do.

MARY. What?

DAVID. She just did it, without any warning. That's how we do these terrible things. We just do them.

*(**DAVID** raises the vial of powder and sniffs.)*

MARY. What's that?

DAVID. Special K. Ketamine.

MARY. You're snorting cat tranquilizer?

DAVID. What?

MARY. Ketamine is a cat tranquilizer.

DAVID. Well, it also can give you perspective.

MARY. You know why they give it to the cats? It's so when you cut into them, they don't think the pain is happening to them, they think it's happening to that other cat.

DAVID. Which is...

MARY. All the same cat.

DAVID. Well, that's what's so great about it. Because it's not me that's running around ingesting cat drugs. It's that other guy. And that fucker's clearly got issues –

MARY. You realize –

DAVID. Yes, that's the point. I totally realize.

MARY. You'll become addicted.

DAVID. That is so...dismissive.

MARY. You've got all the signs: New, secretive behavior. A new person or persons in the subject's life. Abrupt mood swings. Attacking those who try to help or intervene.

(pause)

DAVID. Do you know what I can see?

MARY. No.

DAVID. I can see this guy, who's your husband...And he's right there. And he wants to be good. He wants to be good to you, for you. And he has no idea how.

MARY. That's sweet.

DAVID. No, he wants to be sweet. But he can't be. The best he can do is speak the right words.

(pause)

Richard and Sylvia are coming over this evening. You could stay. Please stay with me, do this with me.

*(**MARY** shakes her head no.)*

What do you want then?

(beat)

MARY. You know what I can see?

*(**DAVID** shakes his head "no.")*

She comes home. She's been doing this for days. Putting her life away in these boxes.

(She gets up, opens a box and pulls out woman's underwear.)

(PROJECTION: "Virginity")

She's been waiting for some sign, for something that let's her know she's done.

*(**MARY** pulls back the small rug near the vanity. There's a blood-stain on the floor.)*

(She lays out stockings.)

Maybe she's calmer than she has been in her whole life. She gets his favorite gun. His gun. She loads it.

(She lays out underwear.)

She sits... She let her him break her nose four times and never gave up. But at this moment, when he's dead and gone, she has a thought, that lets her...surrender.

(She lays out a bra.)

MARY. *(cont.)* Here she is...

(She pulls a beautiful summer dress and a wig from the box, adds them. It's as if there's a woman, lying on the floor.)

Hand up, finger squeezes. Bang. The bullet smashes in, does its work. That split second...All I'm imagining is that split second. Whatever the thought was. Her last thought.

(pause)

That's what I want.

(A box falls from its perch.)

(PROJECTION: "For Mary.")

(MARY goes to it, opens the box and pulls out a pair of worn boxing gloves.)

DAVID. Oh, come on! Is that a joke? That has to be a joke. I mean, I don't believe in ghosts. Do you believe in ghosts?

(She looks up at him for a moment, then gathers her things to leave.)

Don't go. You're out all night. What are you doing out there, Mary?

MARY. I need to walk.

DAVID. You need to sleep.

MARY. Don't talk to me about sleeping. Look at you. You need to sleep. The three of you are like...

DAVID. Then come with me.

MARY. Are you kidding? We can't all be on drugs.

DAVID. You're judging.

MARY. I'm not judging. I just can't go, where you're going. And you can't come with me, where I'm going.

DAVID. It's dangerous out there. And you dress like...look how you're dressed.

MARY. So I'm asking for it.

DAVID. No. Look at you. You don't look like you're asking for it. You look like…you're part of it.

(**DAVID** *goes to her. He pulls off her cap, he touches her face. He sees bruises.*)

What are these?

MARY. What?

DAVID. Bruises. These are new, Mary.

(*rubbing away her make-up*)

Jesus, look at you. How did this –

MARY. It's not what you think.

DAVID. What are you doing?

MARY. You wouldn't even understand. Look at you.

DAVID. No, look at you.

MARY. You're out of control. You've really lost it, David.

DAVID. New, secretive behavior, a new person in the subject's life. Abrupt mood swings –

MARY. This is really pathetic –

DAVID. Mocking those who try to help or intervene.

(**DAVID** *moves at* **MARY**. *She catches him with a punch, sending him reeling back.*)

MARY. David…

(**DAVID** *rises, grabs his satchel, leaves.*)

13. The Gym

(**D.C.** *works the heavy bag.* **DAVID** *comes in, puts down his satchel.*)

D.C. S'up.

DAVID. …S'up.

(**D.C.** *works the heavy bag.* **DAVID** *watches.*)

D.C. Help you?

DAVID. I'm just…watching the whole thing.

D.C. Okay.

(**D.C.** *goes back to the bag.* **DAVID** *moves in a little closer.* **D.C.** *stops, looks at him.*)

DAVID. Sorry.

(*A sudden motion,* **D.C.** *reaches* **DAVID**, *pushes him to the ground, searches him roughly.*)

Jesus, What the hell? Stop! No! No! HELP!

(**D.C.** *finds nothing.*)

D.C. Sorry. Just had this bad feeling about you, man. Sorry, no offense.

DAVID. You do that to everyone who comes in here?

D.C. No, just you. You alright?

DAVID. Yeah. I'm…tuned.

D.C. You're in tune?

DAVID. …Yeah. I'm fine.

D.C. You here to box?

DAVID. Mary Conrad is my wife.

(*beat*)

D.C. (*laughs*) You're lucky. You come in here carrying that in your heart. You're lucky I didn't knock your head off.

DAVID. Thanks. For not knocking my head off.

D.C. How is she? Haven't seen her in a while.

DAVID. She has these bruises, which she covers up. I don't know, why don't you tell me?

D.C.. *(gesturing to his face)* She got one here, and one here. They're nothing. She's tough. Not like when she came in the first time. FUBAR, man.

DAVID. Fubar?

D.C.. "Fucked up beyond all recognition." It's from Vietnam. Anyway, she'll be alright.

DAVID. Fubar.

> *(beat)*

Don't hit her anymore.

D.C.. Her choice, right? I don't make her come here. What you're doing, I get that, that's alright. But it's her choice.

DAVID. Just don't hit her.

D.C.. You know what she called me, the last time she was here? She called me an animal.

DAVID. Her mother died. Recently. So I think she's trying to...destroy herself.

D.C.. Then stop her.

DAVID. That's what I'm trying to do.

> *(pause)*

D.C.. You know, if another man, left a mark on a woman I loved. I'd beat him so hard. I'd just let go on him.

> *(**D.C.** turns back to the bag.)*

DAVID. See, that's the problem, with you people...

> *(**D.C.** stops.)*

You people who work out. You people who practice fighting. I mean, think about it. You practice...*fighting.* Which just screws it up, for the rest of us.

I mean, I'd like to come in here, throw down some kind of glove, we could bloody up each other's noses, mano a mano, maybe go to a bar afterwards. I'd buy you a drink, you could tell me about all your cousins...

DAVID. *(cont.)* But see…it wouldn't work that way. You'd destroy me. You'd really hurt me. How do you think that is, for the rest of us? What have you left us? Lawsuits. Big cars. Money. Fuck you.

D.C.. You want to hit me?

DAVID. God, yes. It's just the getting hit back I don't think I'm ready for.

D.C.. Okay, hit me. Free.

*(**D.C.** opens himself for a hit.)*

DAVID. Seriously?

D.C.. Yes, just be careful of your hand, because –

*(**DAVID** swings at him, sneak attack to the body. **DAVID** howls in pain, he's sprained his wrist.)*

DAVID. Ow! Fuck! Oh, fuck! I hurt my God damn hand. God, I'm just so…I'm just so pathetic. Jesus Christ, what am I supposed to do? What am I supposed to do?

*(**DAVID** cradles his hand. **D.C.** brings him a some ice.)*

D.C.. Hurts like a bitch, doesn't it?

*(**D.C.** stares awkward at **DAVID** who cries on the floor.)*

A little while ago…I lost my house. It was my family's house. I was trying to get a bigger gym. I had gotten a loan on the house.

DAVID. You needed to…

D.C.. What? What did I need?

DAVID. You needed to incorporate. You would have been protected.

D.C.. You see?

(holding up his hands)

How are these, supposed to protect me?

*(**DAVID** staggers up. Moves away from **D.C.**, fumbles in his clothing, snorts K.)*

You should leave.

DAVID. Ever since it happened to her, I've been trying to find a way, to respect myself. But I don't know how.

(DAVID goes to his satchel, pulls out the gun, and shoots D.C. D.C. falls, curled in a ball.)

I'm sorry. I'm sorry.

(DAVID sits. He breathes, long, slow. D.C. breathes fast, hard.)

14. Hospital

(**D.C.** *lies in the hospital bed. Bandaged. Unmoving.*)

(**MARY** *stands across from him, in her doctor's coat. She's holding his chart.*)

MARY. They say you're not talking.
I mean, you can talk, but you're not saying who did this to you.
Thank you.

(**D.C.** *turns his head to look at her.*)

I made a list. Little trick I learned…

(*She takes out a piece of paper. Reads.*)

It goes like this:
First of all, you're going to be fine.
Secondly, it could have been worse.
Lastly, there's me. There's you and me.

(*She drops the paper. Silence.*)

D.C.. My family house burned down, and there was a mistake, with the insurance. I'd go every day, just to look. This time, there was a woman, standing across the street, looking up at my house. I couldn't see her face, but I could hear her. And she laughed. I don't know why she laughed.

(*silence*)

(**MARY** *goes to the bedside. She takes off her doctor's coat.*)

(*She climbs up on* **D.C.** *This is not only sexual, although that's a part of it.*)

(*She pulls the blanket off his torso. Looks down at him.*)

(*She unbuttons her shirt.*)

(*He puts a hand on her skin, under her shirt. She covers it with her own hand.*)

(*They stay that way.*)

15. Home.

(**DAVID** *is standing in the living room. He's got the camera set up on a tripod, with a long trigger cord. He takes self portraits.*)

(*They show up on the screens.*)

(*PORTRAIT:* **DAVID**, *helpless, emotional.*)

(*PORTRAIT:* **DAVID**, *in his undershirt. Hands on head.*)

(*PORTRAIT:* **DAVID**, *in his undershirt. Making muscles.*)

(*PORTRAIT:* **DAVID**, *shirtless. Empty hands towards the camera.*)

(*PORTRAIT:* **DAVID**, *shirtless. Pointing a gun at the camera.*)

(**SYLVIA** *is there, unclear for how long.*)

SYLVIA. Be careful.

DAVID. Ah! Jesus! You scared the living hell out of me.

SYLVIA. Sorry. Be careful with that.

DAVID. What? Oh, shit.

(**DAVID** *puts the gun away in the satchel.*)

SYLVIA. Richard has a theory about this. Fear and sex, sex and death, which in the brain all comes down to there's a thing and you either kill it or fuck it and, well, he explains it better.

DAVID. What?

SYLVIA. And of course if the wires get crossed, then it's like *both* and voila! Jeffrey Dahmer. What happened to your eye?

DAVID. Mary hit me. What are you doing here?

SYLVIA. Photographs. Snap snap.

DAVID. Now?

SYLVIA. Now's better than later so yes now right now.

DAVID. Look, I've had a really weird day.

SYLVIA. Good.

DAVID. No, not necessarily good. Weird and good aren't necessarily –

SYLVIA. You'll like this.

DAVID. Please.

SYLVIA. See I'm going to take everything off and you need to get your camera and you know…shoot.

(*Beat.* **DAVID** *laughs.*)

What?

DAVID. You have no idea.

(**SYLVIA** *pulls her shirt off. Bra underneath.*)

You're okay with this?

SYLVIA. I try not to have opinions about my actions.

(*beat*)

DAVID. I can't.

SYLVIA. Sure you can. What else have you been doing all this time?

DAVID. Trying to…understand my subject.

SYLVIA. Well this will be just like that. Except you can try to understand my tits.

DAVID. I do understand your tits.

SYLVIA. Really? What do they mean?

DAVID. I just mean that they're not…complicated. They're not what makes you…

SYLVIA. You think I'm bigger than the sum of my tits?

DAVID. Yes.

(*beat*)

SYLVIA. Where's Mary?

DAVID. Out.

SYLVIA. Really. For how long?

DAVID. …I'm just saying, that whatever parts you have, like your tits…

SYLVIA. Or my ass. My cunt –

DAVID. I don't think that your tits, your ass, your…vagina.

SYLVIA. Oh, that's a *lot* better.

DAVID. I don't think that if we just took pictures of these things, that we would capture…

SYLVIA. Capture what?

DAVID. You.

SYLVIA. You want to capture me?

> *(beat)*

> Where's "out?"

DAVID. The hospital. The man she boxes with was shot.

> *(beat)*

SYLVIA. Who shot him?

DAVID. He's not telling. Maybe he didn't see.

SYLVIA. Ever since we met you guys, it's like Sarajevo. Have you noticed that? I mean most people say things like "No, I don't care for Carne Asada." But with you guys, it's "my wife was beaten," "mom killed herself," "my trainer was shot." What's that about, David?

> *(pause)*

DAVID. Let's just take some pictures of your tits, and see what happens.

> *(Beat. SYLVIA starts to take off her bra. Stops. Stares at her hands.)*

SYLVIA. That's strange. My hands are shaking.

DAVID. What?

SYLVIA. I don't know. I mean, it's San Francisco after all.

DAVID. Sure.

SYLVIA. When was the last time you felt ashamed?

DAVID. Constantly.

SYLVIA. I don't believe in shame. There's either doing something, or not doing it.

DAVID. That's what makes you amazing.

> *(Beat. SYLVIA starts to take off her bra. Hesitates.)*

SYLVIA. I don't know what my problem is.

DAVID. It's normal.

SYLVIA. I'm not supposed to be normal. Tell me it will be okay.

DAVID. Me, tell you?

SYLVIA. Yes.

DAVID. I don't think it will be okay.

SYLVIA. I didn't see this coming. When we first met you, you looked so harmless. How did this happen?

DAVID. We'll just take some pictures.

SYLVIA. Okay.

(She goes off into the off-limits area of the house.)

Say something!

(SYLVIA's pants fly out the doorway, onto the floor.)

SYLVIA. *(offstage)* You just have to be decisive. You have to say things like "show me your tits."

(DAVID stares at the pants.)

DAVID. Show me your tits.

(SYLVIA's bra lands on the floor.)

SYLVIA. *(offstage)* Good! Try something else. David?

(Beat. DAVID kicks off his shoes. Undoes his belt.)

DAVID. Show me your tits and your ass!

(SYLVIA's underwear lands on the floor.)

SYLVIA. *(offstage)* Keep going, you have to set the mood.

DAVID. Come in here! Come in here and show me everything! Don't leave a fucking thing on because I'm going to take it all! I'm going to take every god damn thing you have to give!

(SYLVIA walks out, dressed in Mary's mother's dress, wearing Mary's mother's wig. She looks beautiful, authentic, from another time.)

(He raises the camera. Click.)

(He sets down the camera. He sits and rests his head in his hands. **SYLVIA** *sits next to* **DAVID**. *She strokes the back of his head.)*

SYLVIA. Shhhhhhhh.

*(***SYLVIA*** leans down and kisses* **DAVID**. *Long and full.)*

(She moves to doorway to the off-limits part of the house. **DAVID** *moves to her, kneels in front of her, buries his face in her stomach.)*

*(***RICHARD*** enters the room. Hair wild, carrying a bottle of champagne. He stops when he sees them.)*

*(***SYLVIA*** sees* **RICHARD**, *holds his gaze for a moment, then raises* **DAVID** *to her, kissing him again, pulling him back with her through the doorway.)*

*(***RICHARD*** stands in the shadows, drinking champagne.)*

(Lights out.)

16. Hospital

(MARY climbs off D.C.. She buttons her shirt.)

(MARY starts to leave, stops herself.)

MARY. I was looking at your house, all boarded up from the fire.

I was going to get one of those delicious wraps.

I saw your home. It looked wounded and sad and empty.

And I laughed, because I saw myself. It was like looking in a mirror.

(beat)

I'm sorry I laughed.

After I got better, I went to a gym, to learn about what had happened to me.

Only what had happened to me, was right there.

I recognized you immediately.

(MARY leaves.)

17. Home

(Early morning. The first rays of sunlight starting to form. The first we've seen.)

*(**MARY** sits in a chair, facing the door to the off-limits part of the house.)*

*(Door slams offstage. **RICHARD** comes in, he has a knit bag filled with groceries.)*

(He turns on the hot-plate, flicks on the coffee maker.)

RICHARD. You have that great Farmer's market on the corner. Excellent. Smell this.

*(He holds out fresh basil and lets **MARY** smell.)*

They grow it out in the Salinas valley. I can pretty much guarantee that this was actually in the ground not more than three or four hours ago. And then someone came along and ripped it out and now we're going to eat the fuck out of it.

(He unloads the groceries on the bed. Onions, Eggs, Sausages.)

Sunday's are the best here. The absolute best. Especially when the sun comes out.

*(**RICHARD** sets a pan on the hot-plate. Then he starts chopping onions.)*

I should never chop onions. I always cry like a mad man. Everyone says pinch your nose or something but it's hopeless.

*(**RICHARD** tosses the onions in the pan.)*

So last night, I found out that they're actually going to publish my book. And I thought: "This calls for alcohol." And I realized that the person I wanted to tell about it, after Sylvia of course. Of course. Was David. Which surprised me, but there it was.

(beat)

RICHARD. *(cont.)* These eggs are from over the mountain. Chickens pretty much run around like dogs and they've never seen a steroid. Oh, are you a vegetarian? Probably not. I'm not, either. I have great faith in complex molecules.

*(**RICHARD** goes back to making eggs.)*

Shouldn't you be at the hospital?

*(**MARY** checks her watch. Nods her head "yes.")*

You look good. You lay off the physical violence for a day?

*(**MARY** nods yes.)*

Anyway. I wanted to tell my old friend David, about how the MAN, the INSTITUTION, had you know, validated me. And I got here.

*(**RICHARD** looks at the doorway.)*

But you know, the timing just wasn't right.

*(**RICHARD** checks his watch.)*

Wow. Seven hours, and with normal liver function plus the milkthistle booster and I'd say…yup. *This, is my brain, not on drugs.*

(beat)

It's actually fairly complicated this way. Because if I have to be honest about it, I'm feeling both a little elated, about the book, and about the morning because fuck if that isn't the sun coming up which in San Francisco is something…

*(**RICHARD** hands **MARY** a plate of eggs and pours her coffee.)*

But at the same time I'm feeling, you know, desperately sad.

*(**SYLVIA** appears in the doorway, still wearing Mary's mother's dress. She stares at **RICHARD**.)*

Anyway, I'm feeling not only these two major emotions but also some little ones. Like regret.

*(***SYLVIA*** *moves to* **RICHARD**, *he intercepts her with a plate of eggs.)*

RICHARD. *(cont.)* You should eat these. They'll get cold.

SYLVIA. *(soft)* I want to go…

RICHARD. You know, just because it's the Bay Area, it doesn't mean I'm not a man. Last time I checked at least. And the problem is I just don't have the context, the you know, context to process emotions like these. These are difficult emotions, to experience.

SYLVIA. Richard…

RICHARD. What? What's the question? Do you want to know the effect you have on my brain chemistry? Am I filled with yummy squishy serotonin when I look upon your cheatin' heart?

SYLVIA. Yes.

RICHARD. Yes. Ah, yes. Big fucking word. They called and said "Yes." We like your words, we like the way you think, man. We're gonna publish you. We're gonna pay you. I don't care if you're a died-in-the-wool red-book-toting Commie, those words feel *good*. And I wanted you to hear them, I wanted you…

SYLVIA. Rocket Twat.

RICHARD. If you say so, baby.

SYLVIA. Rocket Twat. And Ahmed Kahn. Rocket Twat and Ahmed Kahn248! You. Me. I did this for Ahmed Kahn.

RICHARD. Do you know, Sylvia, that half the time, no one has any idea what you're saying.

*(***DAVID*** *appears in the doorway, half dressed. There's something dead, tragically removed in him. He finds his work clothes, puts them on.)*

DAVID. *(quietly)* Ahmed Kahn248…is Sylvia's online lover. Who she believes is you. Ahmed Kahn…is actually a seventeen year- old kid who lives in New Jersey with his parents. I ran a trace. I bought Ahmed_Kahn248 for fifty dollars. It's just the fucking internet.

(SYLVIA *tries to hold* RICHARD, *he keeps her arm's length.*)

RICHARD. No. No, stop it! Get the fuck away from me!

(SYLVIA *gives up, curls on the floor, rocking herself, hyperventilating.*)

…Why?

DAVID. You're so…interesting. Incredible. Amazing. Fantastic. You probably can't even imagine what it's like, for someone who's…not.

(*The song comes on from one of the boxes.*)

That fucking song.

(DAVID *starts opening boxes, wildly looking for the source of the music.*)

(SYLVIA *suddenly moves to the vanity, pulls out the chair and sits down.*)

(DAVID *finally finds the box. PROJECTION: "That song I'm thinking of."*)

(*He pulls an old boom box out and SMASHES it. Beat. The music stops.*)

(DAVID *sees* SYLVIA.)

Don't sit there.

(SYLVIA *smooths her hair at the vanity, makes up her face. She sees herself in the mirror.*)

SYLVIA. Hey…Hey, man. Hi!

(*beat*)

Hey, where's Charlie? Oh, right. Charlie died.

(*beat*)

Yeah, 1964. I was like "give me a guy with a beard and some flower power and I'll open up like a high school girl on Mushrooms." So I didn't see Charlie coming. But I sure fell in love with that man. He was…the most amazing man in the whole world. He was fantastic, man.

DAVID. That's not actually how she –

SYLVIA. It was The Summer of Love, man! It was amazing. And I gave Charlie a baby girl. And I'd hang out in the park, no top on, just pass that baby around. And Charlie and his men, they'd stand in the pool hall doorways, shake their heads. But he had a secret the rest of them didn't know about. He had me, man. And I had him. It was all so incredible.

DAVID. Look, that's not how I said it. She didn't sound like that.

SYLVIA. I know what you're thinking. Yeah, Charlie was an evil sonofabitch. Everyone they'd say "Judy, how do you stay with that evil sonofabitch?" And I'd laugh, because they didn't know everything....

(MARY gets up from her seat and moves towards SYLVIA at the vanity.)

All they could see was a black eye, a split lip. But I could take twice that. I did take twice that.

(beat)

They didn't see him cry and hate himself like his blood was boiling and burning his veins from the inside. But I did. And I decided, that I would just love him so hard, and that all the rest would just be...noise.

(Beat. SYLVIA looks at MARY.)

You could never understand that, could you? Because you were...delicate, tight. If you want to know the truth, I could never really see myself in you.

DAVID. Shut up.

SYLVIA. Always so...suspicious. You would stand there, looking at me, accusing me, for what? For bringing you into the world?

(beat)

Well, the men in your life, they didn't really love you, did they? So how could you understand a man like that?

(silence)

MARY. Hey…mom. Hey…mom.

SYLVIA. Mary.

MARY. I've missed you, a lot. I really have.

SYLVIA. Yeah, I know. I know.

MARY. You make it all sound so great. I wish I could have felt that.

SYLVIA. I wanted you to.

MARY. My husband…

SYLVIA. My husband was –

MARY. *My* husband. I think he fell in love with that…With that story you told everyone. And he thought he could break off a little piece of that world you described, and make it his own. And that little piece of you he broke off, that was me. Can you imagine, how disappointed he must have been?

SYLVIA. You know, if you want to keep a man –

MARY. Hey, I got beat up.

SYLVIA. Makes you stronger.

MARY. Really?

SYLVIA. World's like that.

MARY. That's not what I remember.

SYLVIA. You were only five or six.

MARY. Yes.

SYLVIA. You were tiny.

MARY. I know. But I remember. I really do remember.

SYLVIA. You were so tiny…How could you understand?

(**MARY** *puts up her hand, makes a tight fist.*)

MARY. Look. Look. These curl up, this tucks here. Leave this out, it could break right off.

(**SYLVIA** *doesn't meet her eyes, makes up her hair in the vanity mirror.*)

Do you remember this? Because this is what I remember.

(*beat*)

MARY. *(cont.)* I was scared, all the time. I grew up, scared. And maybe your life was everything you wanted it to be. But mine wasn't. How could it have been?

(beat)

You bitch. Look at me when I'm talking to you.

(Beat. **SYLVIA** *looks over, scared. She tries to hold* **MARY** *'s eyes, can't. She puts up a hand to shield her face.)*

*(***MARY** *takes the hand, strong, pushes it down out of the way.)*

(She kisses **SYLVIA** *on the forehead, tender.)*

*(***MARY** *ends the kiss, moves back a step. There's nothing left in* **SYLVIA**. *She just stares.)*

RICHARD. What just happened here?

MARY. Just a little pretend.

RICHARD. I don't think that's all.

MARY. What else?

RICHARD. That's what I'm asking you. What the fuck just happened here?

MARY. Congratulations, on your book. I'm sure it explains everything.

RICHARD. NO NO NO NO NO THIS WAS SOMETHING ELSE SOMETHING ELSE JUST HAPPENED AND I WANT TO KNOW WHAT JUST HAPPENED BECAUSE I DON'T REALLY KNOW WHERE TO PUT THAT AND I JUST THINK THIS MAY HAVE BEEN A REALLY REALLY BAD TIME NOT TO BE ON DRUGS!

*(***RICHARD** *looks at* **SYLVIA**. *She's not reacting. He comes over to her, close.)*

(gentle) Sylvia…? Where are you? You went far, didn't you? Do you need a voice? Sylvia? All this… shit. This human shit. We're better than that. Or at least, I want to be better than that, with you.

*(***SYLVIA** *jolts up into* **RICHARD**, *kissing him. He kisses her back. Total romance.)*

RICHARD. *(cont.)* Where did you go?

> *(SYLVIA whispers in his ear. He nods. They head for the door. SYLVIA turns back, grabs the camera, takes a picture of DAVID and MARY. This picture remains on the center screen.)*

> *(SYLVIA sets the camera down. RICHARD and SYLVIA leave. Pause. DAVID starts to pick up. MARY is motionless. DAVID stops.)*

DAVID. Mary?

MARY. Hey.

DAVID. Do you want me to stay?

MARY. *(beat)* Yes.

DAVID. I can't stay.

MARY. *(sad smile)* I know.

DAVID. I don't recognize myself these last days. I'm just… Fubar.

MARY. Yes.

DAVID. Okay.

> *(beat)*

You know, I told Sylvia those stories. That wasn't your mom.

MARY. I know.

> *(Pause. MARY sits in the vanity chair.)*

She sat here, all alone, and looked out at these boxes, this puzzle she made. And she thought, *that's* it. When people see this, they'll say "*This,* is what such a woman would leave behind."

Her last thought: "I am interesting. I am incredible. I am amazing. I am fantastic…"

> *(MARY raises a finger to her head, pulls the trigger.)*

DAVID. I think…she wasn't a very good mom.

MARY. …No. She wasn't a very good mom.

DAVID. I think…I wasn't a very good husband.

> *(beat)*

MARY. You wanted to be.

DAVID. Yes. What will you do?

MARY. I'll...unpack.

(DAVID *and* MARY, *staring at each other.*)

(*Behind them, the picture of the two of them, staring out.*)

(*We fade to...*)

18. The Gym and the Gallery

(**D.C.**, *better. He lightly hits the heavy bag.*)

(**MARY** *enters. She's wearing the Barbara Kruger T-shirt "Your Body is a Battleground" $300 sneakers and a ski cap. She's San Francisco hip.*)

(*They stare at each other.*)

MARY. *(beat)* You never said anything.

D.C.. *(beat)* How is he?

MARY. Good. He...took some pictures and it's actually become something for him. He's...found himself here.

D.C.. What about you?

(*pause*)

MARY. Let's just hit.

(**MARY** *goes to her gym-bag, pulls out the old boxing gloves from her mom. She puts them on.*)

(**DAVID** *has a glass of Chardonnay.*)

DAVID. I want to thank everyone who has helped make this exhibit possible. You'll all been so wonderful and I don't deserve this. Seriously, I don't.

(*beat*)

I don't know what I was trying to capture in these pictures.

(**MARY** *and* **D.C.** *start to spar. They duck and bob and hit and retreat.*)

The best I can do is say that I was filled with an emotion that was as big as hunger or lust. I think it is the emotion, of wanting this life to mean something.

(**MARY** *and* **D.C.**, *spar harder and harder.*)

And if you're like me, you have no idea why you're so scared, and why the people around you seem to be so much more than you are. And sometimes, something happens and you get a chance, a glimpse of life. Of really living.

(BAM! BAM! BAM! BAM! goes the sparing.)

DAVID. *(cont.)* So I tried to point the camera, at the glimpse. So I could have it, capture it, take it as my own.

It always escapes. The pictures, are not alive. They're just signposts, that let me know it's still out there.

Anyway, thank you all. I hope you have enjoyed the work.

*(**DAVID** turns towards the photographs. Goes away.)*

*(**MARY** and **D.C.**, still sparring. Good, fast sparring. Rough and enjoyable. **MARY** comes in hard, BAM! BAM! BAM! BAM!)*

End of Play

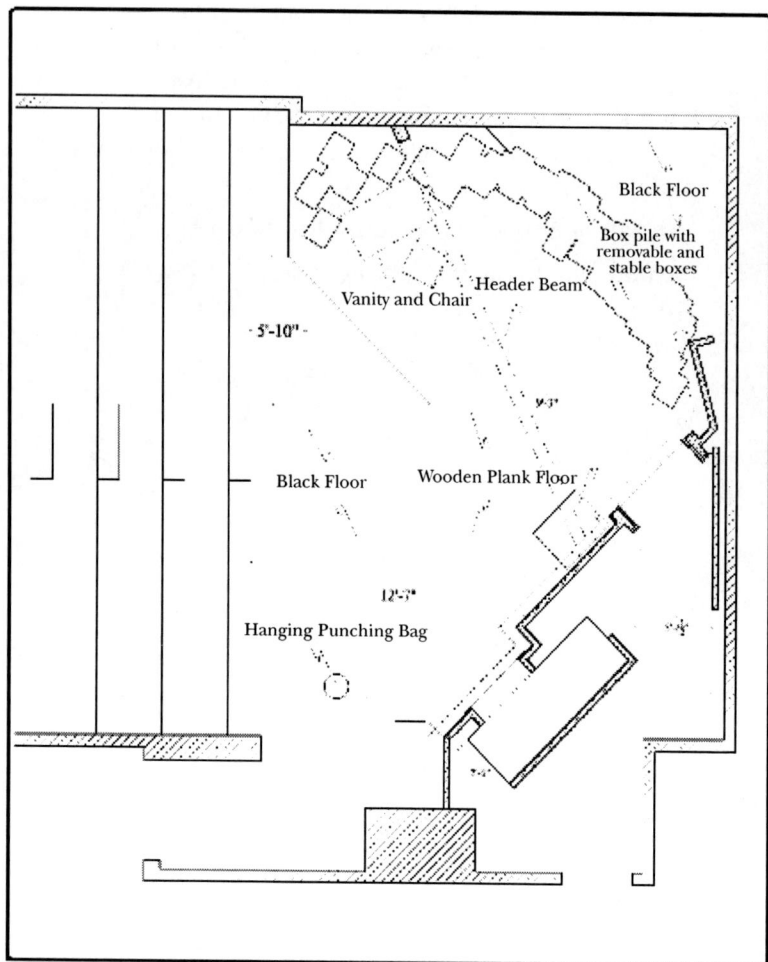

Black Floor

Box pile with
removable and
stable boxes

Header Beam

Vanity and Chair

- 5'-10" -

Black Floor   Wooden Plank Floor

Hanging Punching Bag

GROUND PLAN

Scale: ¼" = 1'0"
Date: 4 May 2009
Director: Larissa Kokernot
Designer: Kevin Judge

CPSIA information can be obtained at www.ICGtesting.com
Printed in the USA
240413LV00001B/6/P

9 780573 697920